Teeth of a Snail

❧❋‖ꞔ **FICTION** *ꞔ‖❋❧*

OSITADIMMA AMAKEZE

kraftgriots

OSITADIMMA AMAKEZE

= KRAFTGRIOTS=

6A Polytechnic Road, Sango, Ibandan

Box 22084, University of Ibadan Post Office

Ibandan, Oyo State, Nigeria

kraftbooks@yahoo.com

(A literary imprint of Kraft Books Limited)

Edited by Amarachukwu Chimeka (SfEP)

amaraobika@gmail.com

Illustrations by Facile Stanley

facilestanley@gmail.com

ISBN: 978-**9181655**
ISBN-13: **978-9789181650**

DEDICATION

To an Unknown delinquent

Acknowledgements

Without you, life would not be worthwhile. While it lasts, make your breath to worth the art of living. The act is that we are made to make earth joyful or full of joy, and not sorrowful or filled with sorrow.

I hereby, acknowledge that life itself has given much; and through whomever life's lessons: bitter or sweet, have added to the subjective *emotitools* appropriated artfully in my literary works, I say a big 'thank you' for making the broth tastier!

You are acknowledged.

Ositadimma Amakeze (Fr.)

Nzudinobieze

Forward

The novelette entitled *Teeth of a Snail* is an enchanting and adventurous tale that calls to mind our African past, when men were still men and women were still virgins; a time when there was still a pathway under the *ukwa* tree. Two major characters are presented in the novel to serve as the microcosm of a macrocosm. They are Udene and Nkuri. Through the eyes and misdemeanors of these two characters we are able to take a walk around the jungle, the village of Umuezike and beyond and by so doing, we become part of many breathtaking, bizarre and dangerous sequences of events that replete the story.

To call Udene and Nkuri two village rascals and never-do- wells might be doing them a great disservice. I prefer to see them as children who are living their lives under the uncontrolled influence of juvenile delinquency. They had only wished to exist, survive and be part and parcel of their environment and perhaps someday, somehow leave their footprints on the sands of time, a feat they both achieved in the end in the most ignominious and excruciating manner. Udene and Nkuri saw the village as all theirs to exploit and they plunged into it. They are just like the proverbial 'child' that was not of age to ask what killed his father, and the same death still lurking in the corner came and claimed the child. Or like the child who was not of age to tie a wrapper and the wind hurriedly came and whisked him and his wrapper away. Sadly, their fate is the sheer fate of a man who dances to the mystic and resonating rhythm of *Sulugede* with little or no knowledge that *Sulugede* is the dance of the spirit. So many proverbs could be employed to describe the person, character and fate of these two unfortunate lads that one will be tempted to go on and on citing them. However, they confirmed the saying that if a man uses *nganga* to swear before an oracle, the oracle uses *nganga* to kill the culprit. The bird, ogazi is such a beautiful bird but it is never used as sacrifice to any deity. All these are lessons gleaned from the exciting and thrilling tale of Udene and Nkuri.

Nkuri is well known as a destroyer, the one who makes the town ripples! His principles and belief in life are enshrined in these words: '...*since things have refused to happen, I have to happen. And if people begin to wonder, then I will begin to wander.*'

These were the words of Nkuri himself. Armed with his bravery and experience in renowned exploits both in the village and the city, he was set to make his mark in the village, forgetting that a monkey can climb and jump so well because trees are close to one another. What then becomes the fate of the monkey when trees are miles apart from one another? The answer is well dramatized in this short but breathtaking thriller.

Udene on the other hand believes that he is forged in the very likeness of the strongest of vultures that has no difficulty in piercing the carcass of a dead man no matter how highly placed or strong he may have been while still alive. Armed with excess bravery and unwavering faith in his exploits, Udene was to partner alongside his cohort, Nkuri to help the writer achieve his tale of doom and destruction. Indeed, it is true that the death that kills a dog never allows it to perceive the smell of dung. Nkuri and Udene forgot that 'gbalagbala felu oke obulu ara.' Their story will now go down the history like that of the legendary Ojadili who challenged his chi to a combat. If not, what else were the two boys searching for in the Amama River on a day the gods were out to hunt for humans to feed their insatiable bellies? Not minding the sea python, daring the deadly reptiles, ominous air of silence and unfriendly nature, the two boys plunged deeper into Amama River in search of what was obviously greater than them. They even had all the time in the world to go to the island to pluck palm fruits, a deed that proved to be the last straw that broke their backs instead of that of female Carmel this time. The gods have limits to their patience and they were bound to strike! Whatever happens next is the inevitable fate of Nkuri and Udene. The story reminds one of the pathetic fate of mortals in his alien world and confirms the saying that we all are to the gods like flies are to the wanton boys, they kill us for their games. Even the snails have teeth and only the farmers can tell the ravages and hurt of their bites. They gods are always ready to strike...

Weaving poetry into lines of prose is exciting. The artist that succeeds in doing this could heavy a deep sigh of relief aware that his work has been done. The critics that will pounce on the work later can only marvel at the level of artistic dexterity and creative ingenuity not possessed by many 'talented' writers. This is what Ositadimma Amakeze has succeeded in doing in this short piece. The lines are so poetic that you can almost sing them. This matters to me above all other things that will definitely capture your attention because the writer has enough fishes in his wares having returned from the 'writer's olu', a place located at the palace of the muse where writing and creativity all began...

I commend Osita Amakeze as I equally recommend this book to all lovers of literature irrespective of class, discipline, areas of specialization, ethnic group, race, colour and country of origin. It is indeed a must read!

Ikechukwu Emmanuel Asika

Writer/critic and author of

'Tamara.'

He drew out the straw, and heavy headed termites clung furiously to its end. Contentedly, he scrapped them into a broken earthenware bowl, brought out more straws from the anthill, and harvested. One red headed termite slit the tip of his left index finger and few drops of blood squirted. He quickly cut free the mandibles with his teeth and smiled at the taste of his revenge. Delightfully, he thought of the savour when his spoils would be fried and eaten with *akpu ngo* at home. The spittle was beginning to dry off. He hastily ran the straw over his tongue and inserted it into the hole again while cursing the inedible brownish ones that occupied one of his baits. Then he smashed them beneath his thorn-torn soles, snuffing life away like trashes in the wind. As he slid his shoulders to the mood of his venture, he heard a tease that made him almost jump out of his skin.

"Agaba n'iduu!" Shouted Nkuri, who stealthily stole behind Udene's back, from a nearby shrub. The sun had lessened its hotness whilst the wind blended with such warmth as between early and late noontide. The pockets of his masquerade-eyed shorts protruded with pieces of stolen unripe pears and pebbles beyond the pocket area. The shorts had obviously been overused. Indeed, the ones loved most by the gods die younger the elders say, and so the cloth earmarked by wear and tear is usually the child's most preferred. On his neck, hung an *nchikiri,* a local slingshot made from an Ogbu tree, a tree which perfectly converges to a confluence at every branch knot. There were patches of dried liquid on his tattered shirt, apparently distinguished by sediments of dirt and sweat. The stench suggested that he may have bathed with *mmanya ocha.* Who would believe that he ripped open a half-full keg of wine atop a raffia palm and used a furled brood leaf to channel the liquid to his mouth as it splattered downward?

The earth abhors things like that!

"Nkuri a na-akurikasi Obodo?" Udene responded from his repressed shock.

"It's isn't easy my brother. If not: why not? Since things have refused to happen, I have to happen. And if people begin to wonder, then I will begin to wander". He spoke with an air of one who had travelled beyond the bounds of Umuezike village. "I retired from township."Nkuri always bragged.

"I wonder o! You are still the same, apart from your big grammar - after all these years of apprenticeship abroad. It is barely a day since you were bundled home from township, and here you are stealing pear and corn, while damaging and ravaging the entire village and farmlands." Udene frowned dismissively.

"Ude, you better ponder and wonder well because the thing that enables the frog to jump is deep inside its belly. Besides the rain, that fell on the leopard did not wash off its spots at all."

"So Nku, you're a leopard? I should think you would rather be a bleating *sheep* having mingled all these while with them in their town"

"See, if you were not my friend I swear, I would have called you *itiboribo*. People who live in the township are not sheep. Though some of them behave like real good sheep, I must say. All they do is climb down from stairs in the morning and climb up again in the afternoon like animals taken from the pen to graze and are led back. Nothing else! Yes, I am a leopard. One that stalks like a lion, scares the tigers and disperses a herd of elephants!"

"That means you are *anumanu?*"

At this, Nkuri grimaced and retorted, "Is that a *compliment or contempt?* Don't add injury to my assault to insult me!"

Scenes of the actual reason for his repatriation flashed before him. On countless occasions, he had eaten the food meant for Chief Ikoro, his boss, feigning that he thought he was dreaming. The other day when he had drained the leftover palm wine at the *Obi*, he had given the same excuse. The seriousness of his claims were enough to convince, or rather confuse one the more that some people could actually dream even while awake. After all it is only a snail that knows what it is to be snail! Only the snail knows why it sighs frequently.

Another day, someone reported that he said he could borrow one of his Oga's wives. As usual, he claimed to be in a trance when confronted by the women who heard it from a neighbour and could no longer tolerate his excesses. The matter was reported to Chief when he returned home. In anger, he put ground pepper in the line that cuts across Nkuri's anus, and dealt his buttocks with hot strokes of cane that were counted to be over thirty-six! Two adults could not have possibly made up such lies. Hence there was no need to hear from the lad. Even if he had not actually said that, it certainly was not far from his misdemeanors. When one poises his hand as if he possesses some powerful medicine, those who have one would of course fling theirs at him to test its potency. A child is not beaten on the day he spills red oil, but on the day he spills unprocessed oil to the ground.

Nkuri regretted coming back to the village. He regretted that he was not guilty of the alleged offence as he had been of the previous ones. Again, he regretted employing his insubstantial excuse of being entranced, but his greatest sorrow was that Ugonne had grossly misrepresented him. People like Ugonne were like scavengers that carried carcasses they did not know who or what it was killed by. Nkuri did not want to borrow anybody. He had only meant to say that he would ask one of his madams for a piece of wrapper when he and Ugonne were discussing about the unusually cold weather at night the previous day. He had been eager to impress and show off that he could now speak "grammar" like his peers, but the borrowed language had failed to convey his native thought.

"At night when cold come, I go borrow one my *Oga* madam to cover me." That was what he said, but what was made of it was not what he meant. Come to think of it, back home at Umuezike, his siblings would be gathered together and covered with an old wrapper on an uncoiling mat soiled with patches of urine. But everyone here claimed to be covered at night with a blanket or duvet. Those words sounded metaphoric to his ears, and his mouth had said what his mind knew.

"It is a dastardly imposition and *Amadioha* will fight them back!" Nkuri comforted himself.

He was still and seemed hypnotized. It was only when his friend tapped on his shoulder and cajoled his somnambulism that he came back to himself.

"Never mind me Udene *ajo anu*!" He tried in vain to cover up, laughing. "You know those in the city dream in the afternoon so they can sleep well undisturbed at night. It has become part of me. Before I retired -though not tired anyway- from Lagos, there were fires burning day and night in the rooms and I could not sleep, unless they put it out." The mention of "dream" again unsettled him but he repressed it.

"Fires inside the room where you lived? Did they pour water to quench it? How did you cope?" Udene questioned with twisted eyebrows itching for quick responses.

"Yes, there were, but small; like *small small* sun tied with twines to some shiny plates or pods. There was even this long one that flashed exactly like lightning. It did not burn but I always did that clapping sound with my mouth to dissuade it from wrecking havoc in the house, for no one knows from where it breathes."

"Nkuri my brother, *ijeru ejeru*. When shall I die to become a masquerade?" Udene daydreamed. "I even heard that the fire makes them drink water that sweats all over its container, which can pull one's teeth with coldness. I wonder o." He continued shaking his teeth like one who had eaten unripe *Oromankirisi*.

"Ude my brother from another mother, the white man is the wonder. Let's move on to where we are going first. I will gist you more, especially about the waters in the house. Water was down in the toilet; water was up in the kitchen. Water, water, everywhere!

There is another one they call *waka*, which sprays water while somebody bathes. We bathed and cooked in the house, ... everything was in the house. Don't worry! On the day of hunting, we shall hunt at the reserve of antelopes for grass-cutters are finished!" Nkuri finalized with a proverb he distorted in iconoclasm.

They walked through the narrow path towards Amama River. Each step widened the greener and succulent leaf-littered path. A wrong location? Yes, they knew but they had not actually stepped out with plans to go anywhere. The tail of a black snake wriggled in swiftly as they approached. It was a rattlesnake! They gawked at each other, hesitated and went ahead. From time to time, a brooding quail freaked, squeaked up and disappeared into the thin air. Its offspring could hide under fallen dried lean leaves, or freeze undetectably. It was amazing the way they did it. The sun was blazing so hotly that numerous reptiles sprayed upon stones and everywhere else for sun bathing. Some spread and slept as if they had been dead for some days. Three alligators were over at some distance. Two were probably male as they were either fighting, probably over territorial sovereignty or making a show of masculine supremacy. They looked stern and very prehistoric!

The lethal slashing of tails of those rival gladiator reptiles, could still be heard several yards into the forest. It was enough to spark off a wildfire!

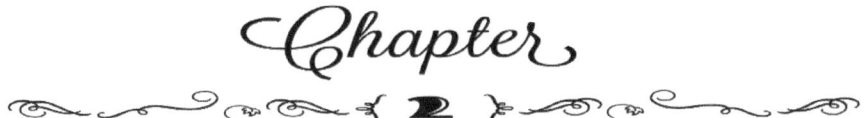

No one dared graze livestock here. Behind the Iroko tree that had stood from time unknown, lifeless though it may seem, was the village pasture plot. Boys who were industrious led their fathers' cows only that far. Protruded stomachs at farmsteads and unending curd chewing told the stories at home. Such boys were rewarded with smoked fish and on some occasions, a little amount of fresh palm wine. There was the case of a young lad who had been warned to not drink to the sweetness of wine but rather to the substance lest it entered his eyes and dazed him. To that he had replied: "I will close my eyes then when drinking so wine does not enter there and confound me." How does one explain that? The proverbial *Ofeke* that did not know when the breadfruit's wood was shared is the same as anyone unaware that an event he otherwise would have wished to participate in was over.

A tuoro Omara, omara, a tuoro Ofeke, o fenye isi n'ohia!

"Look at that python!" Udene who was the more easily frightened of the two feverishly shouted. He clenched his mouth with his fists as if to reprimand his mouth for saying what it should not have said.

"Shsssssh! Silence! You do not see what you think. Yes, but that's *Eke Ogba,* the spirit of Amama." Nkuri replied.

"Is it not looking at us?" Udene asked with his teeth loudly clattering and reminding one of the noise children made when breaking palm kernels over a rustled palm fruit head.

"Hold your breath Ude and walk as if in the dark." Nkuri cautioned half-breathily again. They tiptoed on ahead, wishing their feet did not make the dried leaves rattle so intermittently.

The day was calm except for the discontinuous shrieks of the sacred birds. On a blighted lone branch of a far off tree that stood like death perched an elderly vulture that hid its baldhead across its thighs. It may have been thinking: '*See no evil,*' as the lads trudged on. What people consider a loss is gain for vultures. A vulture whose wife was in labour was asked to pray for safe delivery. Its only response had been "Birth or death, either way is for my benefit."

"Udene there you are!" Nkuri hissed, pointing at the meditating ugly bird intent on diffusing the concomitant tension.

He was about to negate the affiliation, to say his name was not actually *Udene,* when a thick brownish wet cobweb spawned on his face. Spiders do not consider it a problem when any filament of the web indicates the presence of a guest: the bigger, the better. Nonetheless, Udene got what he bargained for because even though the poisonous creature could feel its catch escape, he would scratch his swollen face for as long as the journey into the unknown lasted.

Anyone who will not walk ahead stands the risk of not using his eyes.

From one end of thick gangly branches of varied forestation, monkeys jumped freely from tree to tree. This was the only place where such atypical primates could be seen. Mysteriously, only one among them was translucent. In the sun, it shone like prism; but it wandered in seclusion. It had no brothers or sisters, a mystery no one had yet fathomed. Before the advent of the white man, some folk songs revolved around some monkeys referred to as *Umundu.* According to the lore, these monkeys reflected such beauty and strength, that they were referred to as *children full of life.* How is it possible that a whole generation would go down into the past like a chick in the nest of a hawk? Only this one was left with the rest sediment in folktales. The elders called it *Nwandufu,* the one who misleads. This aberration must be due to a breach in communication, because in the past, it had led many children and even some naïve adults who did not know that its drama of dancing on pathways was intent on leaving them stranded in the thick heart of the forest. That is what was thought. Only the gods know the actual intention of the primate.

Gorillas with noses as wide and deep as the holes where pegs were freshly pulled out and chimps that beat their heavy chests like drums of wars lingered about.

A female chimp had once snatched a baby from a female farmer and held on to it for two days. It fed the baby like it was hers and had refused to let go of it. Sometimes, it chewed certain herbs and squeezed the extracts into the baby's mouth; other times it crushed some wild fruits and seeds to feed the baby. The elders after much consultation with the hunters concluded to plead against the surrogacy but the female chimp always turned her back and climbed up to heights where no man could climb. She also did the same when few women came showing that she knew the gender difference by her actions. While the women looked on stupefied, the female chimp scooped a handful of water gathered from an abandoned hole -possibly made by a Woodpecker- and splashed on her breast. Then she had swiped her nipple severally and slotted it into the mouth of the baby, who had sucked hungrily.

Shooting at her was tantamount to homicide. No matter the precision of the hunter, the dispersal nature of guns put anything close by the target at the risk of getting killed. Life is sacred and blood was left to the gods. No one took his own life, unless he was ready to continue enmity with his ancestors and gods in the other world. Nonetheless, in inevitable cases like wars, or when someone committed a serious abomination like spilling another's blood, he was urged by the community to hang himself. Umuezike would never propitiate for those who died by their own hands.

They even invited Ezemmuo Orishi, who claimed to do all, but his charms had proven to be ineffective. Silently, he rose from the goatskin mat where he had sat spreading his legs over his paraphernalia and left.

Spirits speak in silence in their sureness!

It was on account of such recurring misfortunes and strange incidences that Umuezike named the forest *O mu-uma a cho Okwu*. Hence, he was on his own, who ventured out of curiosity to trespass or traverse this forest. The white missionaries who could not pronounce the name had renamed it *Amama*, the name it eventually came to be known by. Those whites were not afraid of anything. They even camped there in their little magic huts for days. It was also rumoured that they caught lions with their bare hands and sent to their "Elizabeth". Umuezike thought this goddess, *Eliza,* a rather powerful one to ceaselessly demand wild animals for sacrifice! Could this goddess have also demanded *Umundu* and made them go into extinction?

Meanwhile, it was in the early hours of the third day that it was discovered that the chimp had released the baby. She was found foiled in tender leaves and placed under an *Udala* tree near Eke, before the busy market commenced. People usually came from far and near and it was whispered that spirits also came, hence one risked his life by bending his head in between his legs within the market. It was alleged that one man was knocked half dead on a certain market day because he had bent down to pick a twine and in the process looked through his legs. Because it was unintentional, they had only warned him by giving him a lifetime headache.

The people of Umuezu who lived along the riverbank came with canoes and were wealthy merchants. Their houses were built on the shores and even on the water, and they were renowned for catching so many fishes to prepare for a guest as if they had been asked to prepare for a feast. However, no one fished at *Onu Ezu,* an estuary and tributary to the main Ezu River. Many water birds also bred there. It was believed that the deity Ezugolo would strike anyone who fished there. Anything sealed by prohibition from the gods, spirits or deities remained sacrosanct. No one had actually ever seen anyone being strangled by Ezugolo on account of fishing there but everyone believed that someone must have been struck in the past and did not wish to experiment with his or her lives.

Ihe mere ede, o jiri bee nwii!

Indeed, the elders have great wisdom. Just as the cotyledons of a lobe of kola cling together in warmth without any adhesive, so the fear of the gods hold the earth in a perfect poise. If people were allowed to fish at *Onu Ezu*, there would soon be no more fish, because as long as the mouth chews, the jaw would have no rest. It is then appropriate sometimes for men to speak what they will and say that the gods did speak, for the gods would later speak same.

Surprisingly, the measles and rashes on Chinwe, for that was the baby's name, were gone, with her skin looking smoother and healthier like that of a snail. Her mother could not leave her alone at home in her ill state, and that was why she had taken her baby to the farm. Chinwendu, her full name means, "god owns one's life." It is a name that celebrates in gratitude, the providence of one's *Chi*. Indeed there are many mysteries in life. Did the mother chimp know that the baby was sick? If she did, was that why she abducted Chinwendu in the first place, and placed her under natural cure? Could it be that humans were losing it with regards to caring for their posterity? Although there were questions yearning for answers, Umuezike certainly knew that the gods fought for the weak in different ways unknown to mere mortals.

Well, true to Mazi Ufearo's assertion, the secret of good health lies in the forest and vegetation is life itself! A mention of Ufearo would not be enough if who he was, and what he did is left beneath the confines of the tongue. One who climbs an Iroko tree does not climb down in a hurry without gathering sticks to show off. Ufearo was not from Umuezike: he was a native of Umudunu. A man known for his vast knowledge of herbs, and the speeches roots made when blended with water and other roots. His father, a pagan though, was the one who received the other white missionaries called *Ndi Uka Fada* to Umudunu and parceled enough hectares of land for them to build their church. It was a live-and-let-live situation with little conflicts between the two different creeds. Yet, if Udene and Nkuri had agreed to join the white men, they would have trod other paths than that which would eventually lead to destruction.

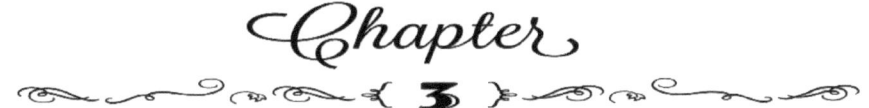
One would think that Nkuri and Udene did not know they should not have trod this lonely path at such a sacred hour? No! They knew. Even as children, they had been informally instructed by folk tales that they were never to go to Amama River, especially at this time of *mgbachi* when spirits and *wilderness* beings rambled about. The seductive river glittered in the sun and beckoned on them to come. Without hesitation they flung their shorts, dropped their wares, and dived naked into the waiting fingers of the warm waters. The death that will kill a dog will first restrain it from perceiving the smell of excreta. The senses are signals of life, the ears hear from the mind and the mind hears from the nose; but they refused their minds to hear the refrain, and instead chose to attend to the urging voice edging them to defile their consciences. Indeed, when two separate voices call a dog to a feast, its head definitely gets stuck in the hole across the fence! They swam like water birds and submerged like crocodiles as if they had been born in the navel of *Onu Ezu.*

"Let's swim to the island and get some palm fruits." Udene suggested after awhile.

"Obi akakwara gi?" Nkuri queried repeatedly to ascertain the strength of Udene's will.

"Why not? Am I not Udene? My heart is strong!"

"Udene kara aka n'amapu ozu afo" Nkuri eulogized, spurting out the water that had gushed into his mouth.

"Yes, I am the one, the vulture that perforates the belly of an adult carcass." Udene boasted in affirmation.

Ihu ogu.... Let's go on.

They swam to an isolated patch of land at the middle of the river and clung on the reeds to climb. It was slippery but where the mind is set, there the body follows. Something stung Nkuri on both hands as he pulled himself up. He neither saw nor knew what it was, but he was sure that he had known pain. In any case, that pain would gain nothing troubling him again because he had only shouted, *"Abia ha,"* and continued picking palm fruits. The boys knew that *Eke Ogba* rested in those parts after swimming and could twirl from the ground to the fronds. They also knew that they were to leave as soon as possible lest the occupant of the lonely colony met them on its way back. So they quickly stuffed their mouths with the fruits and plunged back into the water. When one who is possessed by the spirit of *Agwu*, bequeaths something, it is quickly used up because he might turn back to rescind the offer, if he finds out that it is still available.

Unknown to them, the colour of the water they left a short while ago was not the same as the one they had just thrust back in to. The great lake in Umuezu also changed colour, but not to swallow people.

It was not long before Udene found out that he was whirling all alone. He starred at the vast mouth of the tawny waters and felt the depth coming after him. He stroked futilely, as his widening imagination threatened with all sorts of marine monsters caving in on him. He beckoned on all the gods by names and his ancestors to help.

"Onye kwe, Chi ya ekwe." If one's will is strong, his *Chi's* will in turn support him!

Suddenly, he sighted bubbles dented with oily ripples surge some yards away from him. The seeds in his mouth dropped in successive drooling strings as dangling ripples of water beat gently on his heaving chest to wash the pasty oil away.

"Nkuri!" He shouted as he saw Nkuri make a return from the adulterous bed of Amama.

The fowl says it chuckles insects to death, before it finally swallows. So does Amama, which throws up a drowning victim three times from the deep, before finally ingesting him or her to eternity. No one had ever escaped her amorous grip.

In a splash, Nkuri sprang up as if from the gnawing fangs of the river, with drooling saliva of water all over him. He looked roasted and all of a sudden, he sank back visibly drawn in by some strange strings of forces. Some water forcefully stuck into Udene's ears and drummed. Every single sound magnified and made him feel like his head was bursting.

Udene braved up his spirit. He knew his manhood was useless if he ran away in the face of such trial that would prove his worth as a friend. "I am Udene, the bad meat," he assured himself, beating his thudding chest. "If the eagle claims to be the king of the birds, then I, Udene the vulture, am the king of the king-birds." He was still afraid, but he tried to fight his fears although his clattering teeth betrayed his loose guts. Feverishly, he turned to ward off the swarm of looming crocodiles his imagination had tricked on him.

Sha!

Shaa!!

Shaa shaa shaaa!!!

From a widening dimple that sent ripples to the edge of the bank, it seemed the mouth of the river was gapping "There, there".

Like a cannon shot, the still body of Nkuri rose the second time. Ropes of water clung on him like strings of a strange catapult hitched beneath the earth. Udene sprang as if he had stepped on a stone, but could not save the plunge. He waited as the deep dark mud-smeared body slipped away from his frail grasp. If Amama threw up again and Nkuri was not untangled from her licentious tongue, then he would soon stand condemned before the tribunal of his ancestors. The fly that has no one to caution it, ends up buried with the corpse.

Night was falling upon the earth from the gloomy shades of the sky. The moon and Udene glimmered all alone on the brood face of Amama. He knew now that the dead felt no pains of death and may not even know that they had died. Thus, his heart was now hardened come what may; for one should not be too frightened to fall from a tree because he saw a monkey up there. Yet, Nkuri may still see the moon again if he did not go to the great beyond the third time.

Chapter

4

At home, smokes and flames rose up upon local torches over Umuezike in search of her stray sons. Flutes picked their notes on dirges and swirled to the far away spirit lands, beckoning on benign spirits and calling on the ancestors to help. Mazi Obiefuna knew the flute and the flute knew him. He called the gods by their names with the flute. The spirits make the lad elderly, who begins in his teenage to bear his kinsmen's staff of authority. His late father, who crafted *Oja* all through his life, had taught him how to place his lips on the rim, and heart on the spirits while beseeching the gods! One either goes where his eyes are placed, or sets his eyes at where he is going.

The women went to console Nkasiobi's mother in their usual maternal solidarity. When women wail, they sing their sorrows to the heart of *Ala,* the earth goddess as they recant their *ije uwa*. They solicited their ancestral linage and the gods of the land to come nigh.

Ala doo!

Ala doo oo!!

Ala doooo!!!

The night kept its ears wide. Nkasiobi had been named to stay, live and comfort his mother, Nwoji, as several previous pregnancies had led hopes to the grave.Others had either been stillborn or dead after a few days of birth. She had performed every ritual including fetching from Amama River naked at midnight, so her children would live; but they had all died, all eight of them. She had despaired and refused to take in again. But Ichoku her husband was light in the head, a man who was sure that he had paid the dowry on his wife in full. Thus, one night he had come in and performed his duty as a man, which had eventually led to a pregnancy. Nwoji had moaned through the course, but it was only the few things within her dark room that had heard her. If she had been heard, the elders might have heavily fined her protest.

Ichoku was second to none when it came to jabbering, and that explained why his kinsmen had nicknamed him *Ichoku,* after the parrot. He could talk from when the moon slept till sunset but invite him to work and he would give reasons -like the dung of a duck- why he needed to make a quick exit. Hence, whenever he was sighted in his elements, conferencing with himself towards a folk's compound, the person only needed to lift up a hoe as that alone could make him steer away. He dreaded the farm and farm implements, as oil is frightful of raving tongues of fire. Ichoku did not gossip but only talked about people and events. His real name however, was Ichekeoku.

In her desperation, Nwoji had declined every further ritual

offered or prescribed. Why won't would she, when none had stayed? Anyone who asks a spirit for the fruit of the womb asks for death for no one gives what he has not. We all take off from and return to the earth. People always returned to where they set out from. Even the birds hovering in the sky depend on the earth for their welfare. However, the destiny of a man is charted either by his foolishness or wisdom. No bird is hatched out with a nest on its palms. It only gets a nest when it takes pain, and no rest, till it has knitted a befitting one on a tree of its choice, and at the height of its ambition. Yet, the foolishness of the gods is far wiser than the wisdom of men and their ways are most confusing.

"Woman, bring four matured eggs of a chameleon, and go to a four-crossed road at a sacred hour, and smash them to the ground! Call the four market days; *Eke, Orie, Afo* and *Nkwo* by name that they may know that their fame and name rely on the multitude of children born in front of them." If we all die, the gods will definitely go hungry and perchance die too as no masquerade dances for itself. Let our children live, that the gods will be perpetuated. And this is what *ndu ebebe* means.

No one doubts the oracles; and Ayaka was one *dibia* whose words came undiluted from the gods. The consequence of disobedience was demise -death- which Nwoji would have preferred at that time than the heartbreak of having a baby on one arm, while standing by its grave. The fear that she would die had gripped everyone except Ichoku who thought to himself: "If she lives or dies, Ichoku remains, and I would rather she died than lived, so I can marry Uremma." When an irresponsible man marries a second wife, he recognizes the better of the two. Only the gods knew the deep shrewdness of Uremma's heart, covered with great beauty that had besieged Ichoku's mind to consider divorce or wish Nwoji dead. He had once seen Uremma shimmer during the median outing of the village's *Egedege* Dance; and since then lost his mind on her, wishing he were wealthy enough to marry another woman.

The ninth month came with Nkasiobim, *my comforter,* as insisted by Nwoji. The names given by fathers traditionally took pre-eminence; but it is she who suckles the baby that rules its tongue and what it says. Ask Ichoku the names of any of his children, he would think till tomorrow; ask him to talk and you would have thrown him just exactly where he wanted to fall! He even talked in his dreams while asleep.

Moreover, the gods must have been lying or playing and plying their whims and caprices on the strings of human frailty with demands of this and that! With Nwoji's defiance, Ayaka's fame had gradually died like the dwindling of a smoldering wild fire.

The oracles had ceased.

"Women are evil!" Ayaka would gnash stealthily in confused solitude.

With the recent turn of events, the one whom the gods had earlier sent would be justified. In fact, the gods have their ways of doing things. Nemesis is the fiery arrow that waits at the tail end of the tomorrow of their adversaries, that is, those who deify themselves and thus defy their rulings.

Ichoku's kinsmen went to *Umu-Enyi* to inquire from *Ula*, and the priestess said the gods were angry. They were angry because the woman had refused to offer something they had requested; but this is what they always say, these priests and priestesses. Could it be that the gods needed the eggs of the *ogwumagana* the chameleon this time? One is left to wonder.

These were the thoughts some of his kinsmen considered as they departed alone or in pairs to their homes from their consultation with *Ula.*

Meanwhile, Nwoji was neither comforted, nor did she care for *Ula* and her priestess, Asika. While bare feet marched upon her scarf, she reached for the knot where the lips of her wrapper met, and unfurled it saying: "let the earth behold my nakedness!" She grieved. After all a woman whose only male child is dead is considered naked on earth. Then she had thrown out her hands so that the night would be seen by the curious eyes of the day, but the women had held her close.

"Hold your spirit Mama Nkasi. He will come back before the moon crosses the sky," a voice soothingly assured from the mourners. They had led her into the dim lit red mud hut where she sobbed away in dreams of light and darkness.

Chapter 5

The men had searched in and out of Umuezike and beyond, and while mournfully singing the esoteric, "*A chowa mma ekwu, a na-achocha na ngiga,*" hoping to find them.

Were there footprints of a wild cat, the hunters would have perceived from the moment it entered the land. Otherwise, a lion is not anonymous in the heart of the jungle. Okotogbara would have known from his hut. He could tell every animal apart even in the dark from the sounds of its steps -even rodents. There were still patches of thick bushes and forests though, but the last man, Ogbuagu, who had killed a lion, was now with the ancestors. Hence, it was not possible that one had devoured Udechukwu and Nkasiobi.

If it were when Aguibe's kindred were still incarnating into wild animals, they would have had some questions to answer. Our fathers used them in the olden days as mercenaries of retaliation against warring or rival communities. They were even leased to persons or communities who needed *Odogwu* but did not have. Once they could pay and say who it was that had pointed straight in their face, not minding who was at fault, the other party would be rendered resolutely devastated. These people were also enhanced with potent *Odeshi,* such that neither machete nor local weapons could scratch their bodies. As the days went by, they found that they could will any beast, and take its form to revenge even on personal scuffles. Men died, women got raped and children were displaced.

By the time the elders tried to checkmate them, it was late. It was too late! The lion one sees today was a tender cub the hunter brought home and cuddled as a harmless cat. When a father sends his child on a mission to burgle, he kicks the doors down with two legs! One who did not know he would ever become an *Ozo*, wears the strings of his title up to the knees lest people fail to look down and notice. When a dog gets fed up, he bites even the one that feeds him. The elders…

However, it was Chinweike who had disclosed the secrets of the bat in the noontime. "Since *Egbe Oyibo* found its path in the hands of some villagers, one would be stupid to run the things one uses to scuff his ears in his eyes. These English guns unlike our *egbechakam* are no respecter of *Odeshi.* A single shot alone was enough to make one quickly forget his name, antidotes and incantations. The deaths of Akum and Anum were enough, seeing how bullet holes pierced their throats." A deaf does not need to be told to flee for safety during warfare. He sees that, and on his heels, he scurries!

And that was how the story that a hippopotamus killed Okeke, or lion devoured Okafor gradually died off.

Lions… Yes! Lions roar, prowl and kill only in folktales now or at about some far distant lands farther away from Umuezike's knowledge. Yet, the dried lion's hide, hung in honour of Ogbuagu in his guest hut, rose in Ozo's mind as if the houses were close by. It was a trance. Heavy beaded droplets of blood dripped down its whiskers, as it belched satisfactorily. It stretched to ease, unfurled its paws, winked and opaquely faded as weakness stole him away to sleep. The owl hooted on the *Ogbuchi* sacred tree over his ancestral altar and embellished his dreams all through the night.

He drew his machete from its scabbard, and pulled his dane gun with a grin on his face. He wore a grievous furrow on his forehead, and on his left eye was smeared ash, mixed with water. It was war. The war gong boomed while warriors loomed with their shields and arrows, crouching and stalking some invisible foes. His heart was bitter as the scene of the Umuezike -Ikoro tribal war reincarnated in him. He was his father, and he had had to fight to protect his son, himself. "War is evil," he repeated but would not remove the sacred palm frond clenched in his mouth. Suddenly, an enemy appeared in smokes before him as in the tale of the war Odimegwu told him. He shouted and rose, soaked in his sweat, from his bamboo bed as the assailant's machete tore his left arm!"

"It was a dream, Oh! The gods of my father I thank you!" he gasped in relief, counting his teeth with his tongue. "War is evil," he muttered, remembering Odimegwu his father who had lost an arm in that untold clash. Umuezike had lost men and women to the warriors from Ikoro Kingdom. The women who they took as spoils went with the culture of Umuezike, and till date one hears the names once known of Umuezike people in Ikoro, and sometimes feasts of deities are celebrated in the two different communities on same months. There was even a village in Ikoro called Umuezikeogu. They said their fathers told them that they were descendants of Umuezike and should never forget their names. They invited one another during feasts or festivals.

"But dreams have a way of distorting things," Ozo concluded.

Indeed one's name seeks him in the path of his destiny. Come to think of it! How on earth can a lad named Udechukwu, meaning "the splendor or manifestation of the glory of the great god," prefer to answer Udene, a vulture, instead? Who does not know that Nkuri means, "to destroy, to break, or to devastate?" Certainly, in rituals of giving or taking names, words effect what they say, and when one peeps at the thing that inhabits a hole, he is usually unaware that the thing inside the hole stares back at him!

Ozo knew his son Udechukwu. He knew that one did not ask the he-goat where he slept, but how was its night. Yet, the dream was a bad omen. He remembered the hooting of the owl from the dream. He wished he had his peace and whispered to himself: "His mother can explain better whence he came. Surely that boy is not my blood. And let him thank his *Chi* that slavery has ended." He said that not to betray his fears, for no one gains by losing. No! Not a son! Our children are our wealth, our health and our strength. No one kills his own child. No wise man or woman sells his or her own child! Only a cursed fool could do that even to another's.

In any case, if Udechukwu and Nkasiobi did not return, there would be another ritual burial as seen after the last tribal war, when some warriors did not return home. Trunks of plantain had been wrapped with palm fronds and buried as their corpses. The undertakers had beaten *Ogirisi* leaves all over their bodies to wave death and guilt away from their paths. They had done what should be done; let the gods complete the rest as they deemed fit.

But something happened! Ikuku returned after many years of his burial! At first he had been thought to be a spirit and it took all the oracles to speak, after which he had been reinstalled. Then Ayaka was still influential and considered powerful. He had cut open Ikuku's left palm with a sharp object. When blood spilled, he declared audibly: "Blood is flesh and flesh is blood. *Ikuku ama n'onya!* The great wind that has wings which can never ever be trapped!" That way Ayaka confirmed that Ikuku was not a spirit. Thus no one avoided or dreaded him any longer.

Consequently, there has been less haste in celebrating death in

Umuezike than anticipating life itself. Hope indeed, is the last thing that dies in a man.

Chapter 6

Udene lay bedraggled beneath a wild apple tree all alone. He was not breathing; He was not dead. Nkuri was over the other side of a line, beckoning him to come close, but the further he went, the farther his friend walked backwards. Sadness and sorrows smeared on his face, as he seemed to mutter words like, "Mama m, Mama." While waving his hands as someone in an excruciating pain, he bade farewell to Udene, held his hands on his head and was no more.

The boys had been missing for three days and three nights. It was for two days that Udene had lay there breathless. Apart from the guarded knowledge of few hunters who dared the spirits, the sacred forest of Amama at night was to light, what the secret of the owl, was to the noonday. No one hunted barehanded in the Amama forest. Hunting with local guns, clubs, bows and traps was considered barehanded-hunting. Ikeotuonye was one great hunter, who did not hunt like that, and the crevices of this forest at night and noon knew his footprints. He was believed to have gotten his *Otumokpo* charms from the water spirits. Usually he emerged, deploying his steps, crouching, or stalking, with his headlamp put off. They said he could see clearly in the dark like the cats or bats. Sometimes he perceived a presence from a distance and when he was sure it was beneath a tree; he would draw closer and closer with an eye shut parallel to the nozzle of his gun, while slowly clicking on his trigger....

It was not long after Ikeotu recovered from a shock that he began to hunt again after four years of anguish. He had shot at an antelope one certain night between the boundary that separated Umuezike and Umuezu, but when he came forward, it was a man who lay bleeding from the heart. It was an antelope when he shot it! The elders of Umuezike confirmed this from the hoof-prints that trailed the scenes. Ikeotu had killed a '*mantelope*', not a man, and that was why he was not sentenced to a no-return self-exile. It is an abomination to kill and anyone who killed was sent on Oso *Ochu*. Secondly, the people of Umuezu had been severally warned not to trespass the farmlands of Umuezike as there had once been a clash that had left many injured and crops devastated. The ear that hears must not be as large as that of an elephant's nor should one answer *Okeke-nti-asaa* by name before he learns how to use his ears for the purpose for which they are meant. Umuezu heard, but did not listen. The warnings went through one ear, and left through the other as food in the stomach of one suffering from diarrhea.

It was their forefathers who leased the land at some point in time in the past. Indeed, there is never any trouble in giving a monkey a cup to drink water, but in retrieving the cup. In those days, men gave the hands of their daughters in marriage because *Okonkwo* and *Okoye* were good friends and not because the

44

daughter of Okonkwo loved the son of Okoye. Lands were in the same manner parceled or leased to affable neighbouring communities either in return or request for a favour, or in a bid to sustain friendship. It happened that Ezike, the father of Umuezike gave Ezu, the father of Umuezu a small portion of land when a flood washed away his farmlands one certain year before the planting season. He therefore went with a keg of palm wine to solicit for help, for one's neighbour is also one's *Chi*. After they had eaten kolanut, the men reached an agreement in an unequalled favour to Ezu. He was to pay seven pieces of cowries every year for the eight years he was expected to use the land: and this he had done. Men married a number of wives so as to have a handful of children to work on their farms and make sure the barns were filled with yams, the chief of all crops. The sons of Ezu had walked the distance and worked with their father on that land. Then Ezu had gone to meet with his ancestors, and his sons like a boil growing on the buttock that inflates with each breath, encroached farther on the land a hoe-tongue at a time. Ezike had called his household when he noticed that the handshake was going beyond the elbow and had told them to stand as his strength was failing. He also took his first son, Ezika to the land and showed him the landmarks and edges of the boundary.

"You see that giant Ukpaka tree over there; it was the height of an adult he-goat when Ezu stopped paying me. I tell you this so you can say your father told you and not because I want you to demand payment from his sons because they don't have either. Besides they do not have enough with which to pay. It would be like asking palm kernel to provide red oil. Yet, since oil is what is needed, let them lay off their hands from this land."

It was not long afterwards before Ezike passed on in peace. Within the month-long burial rites and ceremonies, Umuezu swiftly scrambled the land like hungry chickens that suddenly discovered an anthill. The elders of Umuezike sent words but were ignored as the elders of Umuezu feigned ignorance. Even though they knew the truth, they sat on it and allowed their youths wallow restlessly in danger!

It was when the farmland got fenced with sticks and palm fronds from one end to the other, cutting off the views of Umuezu that the tune of the dance had changed. Every morning it was discovered that an arm of the fence was felled the night before, or that crops were scathed beyond survival. No human being could have done that: thus for a long time no one was held responsible. One either saw footprints of Ozodimgba, the warrior Chimpanzee or wreckages only an angry wild pig could possibly cause.

However, the age long ravages of the farms of Umuezike at night, by irate beasts instantly ceased with the story of a hunter who killed an antelope that had turned a *man.* Umuezu now knew why no more warnings came at their defiance, or they supposed that the onslaught was the response of Umuezike's silence.

Umuezike did not know what happened, *so Chukwu maru!*

Meanwhile, when an ant stings the buttocks, it learns to sit with caution, and one does not hang a stone with a string over his neck because of his fame at eating palm kernels. Hence Ikeotu held his breath and the trigger, while flooding his headlamp with the nozzle of his gun ready to explode. Lo and behold it was Udechukwu! Strangely, he let the trigger loose over the air and hot ashes, pebbles and pieces of metal perforated the leaves and trees in the cover of the dark. *"Okike doo!"* Ikeotu gasped.

Udechukwu who was awoken by the deafening explosion shrugged, but everything was in white as if the sun shone directly in his eyes. He wanted to shout, but he had forgotten how to: he remembered nothing. He struggled to know where he was, to ward off the light, and or to run away, but could not move for numbness ran through his bones and nerves. Blinded and despaired, he went unconscious again.

How would a hunter take home an unconscious lad instead of a deer, grass-cutter or any other game, without being reminded of the horrible past? Ikeotu looked at the clouds, the early morning cock had not crowed and the moon was yet to cross. One does not pull the whiskers of a live lion without getting hurt. Nothing escaped the watchful eyes of the villagers at any time, apart from those hidden away by taboos and customs. Wine tappers told tales of dawn, drunks told that of day and dusk, while night guards who kept vigil till dawn knew what transpired between the living and the dead. However, not the type, as the story was told, of a night guard who told his Oyibo boss not to go out one certain day, as he would be abducted from the dream he dreamt. He even said he struggled with about five hefty men the previous night, who succeeded in escaping with his gun; when he could not find it in the morning. Those men had come for his master, but since they didn't make it, would lay ambush were he to set out that day. That was the day he lost his job.

So Ikeotu found himself in a dilemma. If he carried the unconscious lad home, only the gods would know that he had not shot at another man, but that was not enough. Humans should also know, not only the gods. In this difficulty, he searched for herbs with resuscitating potency. *Ogirisi* has such powers, but was rarely found in the forest. The wild newbouldia if found, has shrunken and smaller leaves than the breed used in building fences, barns, and setting out boundaries at home. Silently he prayed he would find one quickly.

The day had gradually awoken from sleep and concealment of the dark. He met a few wine tappers going home or straight to the market with fresh wine; and a couple of farmers who must have come earlier to check their mounds or make new ones before the sun descended upon earth in restraining hotness. One saw him and quickly diverted to the path that led to Amama shuddering in reverence. By the time Ikeotu returned, there were some vultures perching and hovering over the tree where Udechukwu lay lifeless, waiting to be sure that he was emptied of life. Ants had infested his log of flesh and were walking through his nose and mouth! Ikeotu picked his gun from where he had abandoned it and scared the vultures away with a shot. Then he beat off the insects furiously and fanned Udechukwu with the herbs. He squeezed the seven pieces of leaves, wrung it and let the dark-green extract drip through his nostrils. Anyone who does not wake within the time *Ona yam* is cooked and done is considered dead.

Udechukwu did not die. His spirit came back slowly like a seedling sprouting through earth. His eyes opened to the sun. He was given water, and he sank it like dried desert sand. Ikeotu shot dead a squirrel with his catapult and roasted. It must have thought it was safe to toil, since it walked into the death trap itself. Udechukwu ate everything as if the poor rodent had no bones. It was time to walk home. He trudged and Ikeotuonye stalked him while they walked. He knew that the sacred hour of *mgbachi* would come before noon and that they must set their feet behind the ambience of Amama lest they meet with spirits. The elders know this.

"Where is Nkuri?" Udene blurted like an unprepared rain eventually. He heard no answer and he was not expecting any. He would have received one though, if only he breathed in another bout of strength.

Like a wild fire that starts here and stretches there and everywhere, rumours rose to spread that the boys had been found. People ran to the village square to see. Someone quoted another, who said that someone else said he saw the both of them with his eyes! Everyone soon heard this version amidst many others that were too numerous and scary, and they prayed it was so.

Whose voice could one hear in the uproar? Mazi Okwundu kept on raising his hands to heavens with mere mutterings as he gazed at Udechukwu. It was just few days ago that he had warned Nwabunna his son, to desist from the company of Nkasi and Ude. "When the goat that does not eat cocoyam goes with the one that eats cocoyam, sooner or later, it begins to eat what it has not been eating," he sternly warned his son. It would have been a different story if Nwabunna had not heeded his father's reproach. Indeed, the thing an elder perceives or sees while he sits cannot be seen by a youth even if the youth climbed the tallest of trees.

Udechukwu barely had enough space as the crowd surged forward on him. He could not hear their voices: the only sound that he heard was that of the turbulent Amama River. Furthermore, he also could not see the people: the only thing he saw was Nkuri plunging the second time. He did not remember any other time. The python had unexpectedly driven in its head from the bank of the river, just as he had resolved to rescue his friend on the third emission. The last thing he remembered was how swiftly he had sunk! Had Nkuri come out again? He did not know, neither did he know how he had come to sit beneath the wild apple tree. Udechukwu had forgotten everything including his name.

 Epilogue

Those who place sacrificial items go out at night in order to evade the probing eyes of the day. Sacrifices are made to spirits on pathways especially on crossroads, riverbanks and everywhere else that the spirits for which the offerings are intended are likely to pass. Sometimes, people from other villages are directed to go to another village where there is a more powerful deity to offer their sacrifices to. Yet, it must be of grave cause for one to go down to Amama for a ritual, especially at late or early hours. Such was the reason for which an unknown stranger clad in the cover of night went to Amama. He had dumped the prescribed items; a goat strapped to silence with black, white and red cloths; forty-eight pieces of cowries; a white chick, and four eggs placed in a rough little basket. The number of ritual items is not arbitrary, but symbolically chosen for specific reasons and effects. When the stranger saw a floating figure not far away from his canoe, he was frightened, thinking it was *aguiyi*. Those monstrous reptiles were sacred totems in Umuezike, and as such were never killed, but they did kill. They could track a fisherman from beneath his canoe for hours till it was safe and sure to strike. Hence, he kept calm like a floating log of wood, till he noticed it was no crocodile but a drowned person.

One can turn his back to a feast, but not to a dying or dead man.

In the face of two necessary evils, one chooses the lesser one. Udechukwu had reflexively chosen to stay beneath the waters of Amama, than in the abysmal belly of the retiring python. He was lucky that the python had not seen him. He had held his breath till he breathed no more and was later washed afloat. There were white gashes on his body showing that the fishes had counted his nerves and could not wait to share his flesh once it started decomposing. Indeed one's state of mind when he is awake propels his mind and body even while he is asleep. Udechukwu had refused to despair, even when he should have, thus the gods had not given up on him. Where Nkuri was, he could not explain. In fact, there are many things one cannot explain in this life, many mysteries and their myths. Yet, if one does not know what is done, he is used to doing what is being done!

At nightfall, the village square stood deserted as pathways led people from where they came. Only two families, close friends and relatives or enemies stayed in the dark to see to its end. Some held their hands on their breasts, some clung onto their arms; some stood with hands on their waists while walking and stopping as if hypnotized. When a man lays his hands on his head, know that *aru mere!* An abomination or some kind of misfortune had indeed happened or befallen him.

Where is Nkasiobi? No one knew. Udechukwu, who could have

told, had no speech. He did not hear their voices as he still heard only the turbulent waters; he did not see the people as he still only saw Nkuri plunge the second time. He did not remember any other thing, not even his name, as his mind had become haunted. They bore him home like a lame, hoping the gods would restore his tongue.

It is with its tongue that the snail sails through thorny stocks. Yet, when snails inhabit a farmland, slowly, indeed unhurriedly, the farmer would soon come to reckon the ravages of the, "Teeth of a Snail."

"Tomorrow, we shall go and inquire," they said.

If only the gods would speak.

 Glossary

Nganga	-Pride
Gbalagbala felu oke o bulu ara	-Hyperactivity is prone or close to madness
Akpu ngo	- Tapioca
Agaba n'Iduu	- Warrior
Nchikiri	- A local slingshot
Mmanya ocha	- Palm wine
Nkuri a na-akurikasi Obodo	-Portraying Nkuri's destructive tendencies.
Itiboribo	- A dullard
Anumanu	- Animal
Obi	- General council room
Oga	- Boss
Amadioha	- The Sky god, speaks through thunder; also known as god of thunder
Udene ajo anu	- Vulture (Bad meat)
I jeru ejeru	-You're right on spot
Oromankirisi	- Lime

Waka	-Spreading on fingers in contempt; even though Shower is meant
Ofeke	- Fool
A tuoro omara, o mara, a tuoro ofeke, o fenye isi n'ohia	-The wise heeds to good advice but the fool basks in his foolery.
Eke Ogba	- Python
Udala	- Native African apple
Ihe mere ede, o jiri nwii	-The cocoyam stalk does bee not squelch for nothing
Chi	- god
Mgbachi	- Mid afternoon
Obi akakwara gi?	- Are you brave enough?
Udene kara aka na-amapu ozu afo	- The vulture that perforates the belly of an adult carcass
Ihu ogu	- War front
A bia ha!	- They have come!
Agwu	- Spirit of misdemeanour
Onye kwe, Chi ya ekwe	- One's personal god consents with his will
Eke, Orie, Afo and Nkwo	- Market days
Dinta chowa egbe ya, o na-achocha ma na ngiga	- A hunter looks for his gun , even in the most unlikely places
Odogwu	- Warrior
Odeshi	- Charm to prevent harm

Ozo	-The highest traditional title taken in Igbo land
Egbe Oyibo	- English gun
Egbe chakam	- Local gun
Ogirisi	- Newbouldia Shrub
Ikuku ama n'onya	-The wind that cannot be trapped
Aguiyi	-Crocodile

Summary

Indeed one's name seeks him in the path of his destiny. Come to think of it! How on earth could a lad named Udechukwu, meaning "the splendour or manifestation of the glory of the great god," prefer to answer Udene, a vulture, instead?

Who does not know that Nkuri means, "to destroy, to break, or to devastate?" Certainly, in rituals of giving or taking names, words effect what they say, and when one peeps at the thing that inhabits a hole, he is usually unaware that the thing inside the hole stares back at him!"

Thus, it is with its tongue that the snail sails through thorny stocks. Yet, when snails no matter how small or big inhabit a farmland; slowly, indeed unhurriedly, the farmer would soon come to reckon the ravages of the, "Teeth of a Snail."

"Those who assume that the "teeth" of the snail of their conscience has no bite, will always end up standing in the midst of moral ruins after all the ethical fibres of their being have been rasped and scrapped away by wrongdoings"

- Emeka Amakeze
Nollywood Filmmaker

 About The Author

Ositadimma Amakeze has read. He is still reading as he strives to attest the difference between certification and qualifications through art. As an artist and poet, he talks about the Muse more often than not; as evident in his poetry book, "The Blazes & Buzzes of the Muse."

The demiurgic force as it were, fashions the sensible world of his words through the walls of eternal ideas. As such, the ethereal eloquence and ingenious exploitation of events found in his novel "The Last Carver," and other works of his, testify to a sublime possession of thought wrought in a conscious silence and solitude of being!

The contention above stated, such as seen in the two protagonists in "The Teeth of a Snail" is a flawed phenomenology, *"..., since things have refused to happen, I have to happen. And if people begin to wonder, then I will begin to wander".*

He believes 'we happen' but there's an ethics that guides such manifestation. Thus, it is wrong to assume there's no wrong in doing things wrongly. The two delinquents did...., *"One would think that Nkuri and Udene did not know they should not have trod this lonely path at such a sacred hour? No! They knew. Even as children, they had been informally instructed by folk tales that they were never to go to Amama River, especially at this time of mgbachi when spirits and wilderness beings rambled about."* And they were done!

Indeed, everything perceived is possible, but not everything conceived is permissible.

The author is the founder of YOWAMCA (Young Women & Men Creative Association) whose motto is, "Creativity Without Borders!"and a vibrant book club, O'star Book Club that believes in, "Teach a child to read good books and write right, and save the world tons of troubles."

Ositadimma is a member of Teachers Registration Council of Nigeria (TRCN), Association of Nigerian Authors (ANA), and Member, Nigerian Red Cross Society.

Above all, he is a Catholic priest of Awka Diocese; and native of Nimo, a people with unique names in Anambra State-Nigeria.

Nzudinobieze

www.ingramcontent.com/pod-product-compliance
Lightning Source LLC
Chambersburg PA
CBHW041032170626
46815CB00005B/290